D0819613

The Stray

Written & Illustrated by

MOLLY RUTTAN

 Nancy Paulsen Books

To all the strays in this world and beyond . . .
and to all the homes that make room for them.

NANCY PAULSEN BOOKS
An imprint of Penguin Random House LLC, New York

Copyright © 2020 by Molly Ruttan
Penguin supports copyright. Copyright fuels creativity, encourages diverse voices,
promotes free speech, and creates a vibrant culture. Thank you for buying an authorized
edition of this book and for complying with copyright laws by not reproducing, scanning,
or distributing any part of it in any form without permission. You are supporting
writers and allowing Penguin to continue to publish books for every reader.

Nancy Paulsen Books is a registered trademark of Penguin Random House LLC.

Visit us online at penguinrandomhouse.com

Library of Congress Cataloging-in-Publication Data
Names: Ruttan, Molly, author, illustrator.
Title: The stray / Molly Ruttan.
Description: New York: Nancy Paulsen Books, [2020] |
Summary: "A family tries to adopt a stray alien,
with unexpected results"—Provided by publisher.
Identifiers: LCCN 2019018205 | ISBN 9780525514466 (hardcover: alk. paper)
| ISBN 9780525514497 (ebook) | ISBN 9780525514473 (ebook)
Subjects: | CYAC: Extraterrestrial beings—Fiction.
| Pet adoption—Fiction. | Humorous stories.
Classification: LCC PZ7.1.R93 Str 2020 | DDC [E]—dc23
LC record available at https://lccn.loc.gov/2019018205

Manufactured in China by RR Donnelley Asia Printing Solutions Ltd.
ISBN 9780525514466
1 2 3 4 5 6 7 8 9 10

Design by Suki Boynton
Text set in Minou
The illustrations were brought to life
with charcoal, pastel, and digital media.

Yesterday morning . . .

we found a stray.

He didn't have a collar,

and he didn't have a tag . . .

so we brought
him home.

We named him Grub.

We thought we could teach him a few things, like

SIT!

STAY!

DOWN!

COME!

But it turned out . . .

he wasn't even housebroken!

So we took him for a walk.

He seemed to enjoy meeting the neighbors!

When we got home, Grub settled down. We thought he would be happy being part of our family!

But it turned out . . .

Grub didn't seem to be happy at all.

We wondered if it was because he already had a family somewhere else.

But we didn't know
where in the world
they could be.

So even though we didn't know where to look for them, we tried our best to contact them.

We thought they might
be impossible to find!

But it turned out . . .

They found us first!

We were sad Grub had to leave,
but it felt good to know he was happy
and was back with his family.

And who knows?
Maybe we'll see him again
sometime!